Surf's Up, SpongeBob!

by David Lewman • illustrated by Heather Martinez

SIMON SPOTLIGHT/NICKELODEON
New York   London   Toronto   Sydney

Stephen Hillenburg (signature)

Based on the TV series *SpongeBob SquarePants*® created by Stephen Hillenburg as seen on Nickelodeon®

 SIMON SPOTLIGHT

An imprint of Simon & Schuster Children's Publishing Division
1230 Avenue of the Americas, New York, New York 10020
Manufactured in the United States of America
10 9 8 7
ISBN-13: 978-1-4169-7869-5
ISBN-10: 1-4169-7869-0

"HII-EEE-YAH!" SpongeBob yelled as he lunged toward Sandy with a mighty karate strike.

Sandy easily blocked his attack. "Nice try, SpongeBob," she said, chuckling. "I think that's enough karate for today."

SpongeBob nodded. "Same time tomorrow?" he asked eagerly.

Sandy shook her head. "No can do, SpongeBob. I'm going to be grabbing my stick and carving some barrels!"

"Huh?" SpongeBob asked. He had no idea what she just said.

"I'm going surfing!" Sandy explained. "Wanna come?"

SpongeBob hesitated. "Well, I don't know . . ."

"You may be a beginner, but I'm excited to teach you to surf," Patrick explained. "That was surfer talk."

SpongeBob looked surprised. "You know how to surf, Patrick?"

Patrick smiled. "Of course I do! Why do you think I wear these cool surfer shorts all the time?"

"Because they're the only pair you own?"

"Exactly! Let's go!"

At Goo Lagoon, Patrick began SpongeBob's first lesson. "The first thing you do is—"

"STAND BACK!" shouted Larry the Lobster. The big lifeguard set a groaning surfer down on the sand.

"Wh-what happened?" SpongeBob asked anxiously.

"Dude tried to catch a bomb but ended up getting drilled in the zone," Larry replied seriously.

"Huh?" SpongeBob asked.

"He tried to surf a wave that was too big for him," Patrick explained.

Trembling, SpongeBob suggested, "Maybe we should leave."

"Why?" asked Patrick, puzzled. "Are you scared?"

SpongeBob put on a brave face. "No . . . I just don't want to run into Sandy."

Patrick shrugged. "Okay, I can teach you right in your own yard."

Back in SpongeBob's yard, Patrick laid his surfboard on the sand. "Okay, lie down on your stick," he said.

SpongeBob looked around. "But I don't have a stick, Patrick."

"That's what we surfers call our boards," Patrick said.

"Oh, right!" SpongeBob said. He lay down on the surfboard like it was a bed.

"Good!" said Patrick. "Except you're supposed to be on your stomach."

SpongeBob turned over. Next Patrick showed him how to paddle out to a wave, pop up, and stand on the board.

After a while SpongeBob started to get the hang of standing up on the surfboard. "I think I'm getting it, Patrick!" he said, excited. "You're a great teacher!"

Patrick smiled. "Now you just have to try it on a wave."

"Where do we get a wave?" SpongeBob asked.

Patrick thought for a moment. Then he snapped his fingers. "I know! Squidward's bathtub! Come on!"

In Squidward's bathroom Patrick called out directions. "All right! Now try a cutback toward the lip! Catch some air!"

When Squidward came home he was a little upset.

"SURF'S UP!" Sandy shouted as she charged into the water with her surfboard. "Come on, SpongeBob! I can't wait to hang ten!"

"Yes, Sandy, I also want to curl my toes over the front of my board," SpongeBob answered, proud to know what she was talking about. He took a deep breath and was about to follow Sandy when a surfer dragged himself out of the water.

"How is it out there?" SpongeBob asked.

"Awesome," the surfer answered. "And terrifying."

SpongeBob gulped. "Are you going back in?"

The surfer shook his head. "Not happenin', dude. Broke my board."

As the surfer walked sadly away with his broken surfboard, SpongeBob got an idea.

SpongeBob jumped up and down on his surfboard. If I break my board, then I *can't* go surfing! he thought. I'll be saved!

But the surfboard didn't break. "Hmm . . . this stick is tougher than I thought," SpongeBob said, stomping hard.

As he jumped, SpongeBob looked out for cracks on his board. He didn't notice that his board had slipped into the surf, and that he was being carried out toward an enormous wave!

"If I can just jump hard enough, I can break this stupid surfboard!" SpongeBob said. He had no idea that he was riding the biggest wave to ever hit Goo Lagoon!

SpongeBob kicked the surfboard. He tried standing on his hands and pulling at the tip of the board. He punched, smacked, and whacked the board—but nothing worked. This was one tough surfboard!

Finally SpongeBob gave up. "I'll just have to tell Sandy the waves are too big for me," he said, before looking up to see . . .

. . . a huge crowd on the beach—cheering for him! Sandy ran up to SpongeBob. "SpongeBob, that was fantastic! Nobody's ever ridden a wave like that before!"

"Ridden a wave?" SpongeBob asked, confused.

"You rode that humongous wave like a cowboy on a buckin' bronco!" Sandy said, grinning from ear to ear.

"I did?" SpongeBob asked. "I mean . . . yeah, I did!"

"Hooray for SpongeBob!" everyone shouted.
"Hooray for gnarly waves!" SpongeBob shouted back.